Charlie's

Great Adventure

by

C.A. GOODY

illustrated by

TERRY LAAKER

To Presley –
Love & Blessings,
CA Goody

Cover design by Reid Johns
Written and Printed in the U.S.A.
Typeset and Printed by TKPrinting

Copyright (c) 2000 by C.A. Goody

First Printing July 2000
ISBN 978-0-9702546-4-1

Goody, C.A. 1962-
Charlie's Great Adventure, C.A. Goody

Summary - A kitten adapts to life with a human family, then gets lost and must find his way back to them.
1 - Animal Adventure   2 - Cats   3 - Humor   4 - Kittens

ACKNOWLEDGEMENTS

*My thanks to Barry Spilchuk and Diana Loomans,
for encouraging me.*

*Thanks to Cheryl Mertz, Wendy Reiner, Kathleen Hudson,
Alta Chapin and Fran Swartzwelder who helped
with editing and support.*

*Special thanks to Ken and Ruby Byrne
for believing in me.*

TABLE OF CONTENTS

Chapter 1

Meet Charlie

Hi, MY NAME IS CHARLIE. I'm an Abyssinian cat. Pretty fancy title for a house cat, don't you think? Basically, it means that my ancestors all looked pretty much like I do. People say I look like a mountain lion with a pussycat's face. We Abys go way back to the time of the Egyptians. Did you know that some Egyptians treated cats like gods? It's true. In my fantasies, I can see one of my distant relatives modeling for the sphinx, but in reality, they were more likely in charge of keeping the mice out of some stonecarver's shop.

But enough history. This story is about me and my adventures. It all started when I was just a little kitten.

My mom lived on a big ranch in the hills of Northern California. I was born in the barn there. I should explain here that this was no regular, run of the mill barn I was born in. The lady who owned the barn raised special horses there.

These were very rare show horses, so the owners spared no expense in pampering them. The barn had special heaters for the winter, air conditioning for the summer, and classical music was piped in day and night. My mother was a show cat and spent most of her time living in the house, but she believed it would be better if we were born and raised in the barn. She told us it was so we could listen to the music all day and develop not only our natural cat grace, but a good sense of rhythm, (Although I believe now that it may have had something to do with the fact that Mistress hated the house getting messy. You know how rowdy a group of kittens can be).

So, I grew up in the barn. It was a great place. The horses were friendly, it was warm and cozy, and Bach, Beethoven and John Phillips Souza were my constant companions. There were just four of us in my family: Mom, my two sisters and me. Being girls, my sisters weren't a lot of fun to play with. Every time I wanted to practice pouncing, they would want to practice cleaning and would wash me all over. Yuck. When I wanted to play 'Got your tail,' they would practice being finicky and just ignore me. So, I began looking for other friends, and I found one in Clarise.

Clarise was an old horse who had lived in the barn for many years. In fact, she was the oldest animal on the farm (other than a turtle who lived under the oak tree and claimed he was over 100). Clarise would never admit how old she was, she would only say that she could remember being the only horse there, and that the music and air conditioning had been put in for her. We made sure to thank her during those hot, late-September afternoons.

Looking back, I'm not really sure why Clarise was willing to be my friend. I was a tiny kitten full of energy and looking for trouble, while she was a tired old horse looking for peace and quiet. But for some reason, she decided not only to put up with me but to take on the task of educating me as well.

"All animals should have a basic understanding of reading," Clarise told me. "It is then possible to understand humans a little better. They will never understand us, and since we must live with them, it is to our advantage to comprehend them as much as possible.

"The Great Creator of All Life gives each of us a special purpose," she continued. "For many years, I thought my only purpose was to be beautiful and win horse shows. But as I got older, I realized I had a special gift for understanding humans. The more you know about people, the easier it is to love them. And people need love more than anything else. Now I wish to pass this special knowledge on to others."

She started me with the ABCs and basic phonics. By the time I was 5 weeks old, I could read a few of the words on the crates inside the barn, and by 6 weeks, I could read all the food bags. My mother was quite impressed, but my sisters always complained when I told them what was actu-

9

ally in the food they were eating, and the other animals in the barn informed me that I would no longer be welcome to sit with them while they were eating if I read their food labels out loud ever again.

When I was six weeks old, my mother told me it was time I got a place of my own.

"A cat needs his own space," my mother explained. "People like to have cats around, because we add an air of grace, beauty, and fun to any home. In exchange, they give us food, shelter, love, and just about anything else you can ask for. The trick is to get them to understand you. Humans have a very strange language, but they can be taught to understand enough 'meows' for you to get your point across to them. Just be patient. Eventually you'll be able to train whatever family you choose."

Choosing the family was easy. One day, Mistress brought a little girl into the barn. The girl was the granddaughter of one of Mistress's friends, and she wanted to see the horses. I'll never forget the first time I saw her. Beethoven's Seventh Symphony, my personal favorite, was playing in the background, when this small human with long golden-brown hair and blue eyes walked in. She was wearing this small, shy smile on her face as she looked at the horses. They were much bigger than she was, and I think she was a little afraid of them. But when she spoke to them, it sounded almost like singing, and the horses started smiling shyly too.

Then she looked at me, and a huge smile broke out all over her face. It felt like the sun had just come out, and we were still inside! It made me feel all warm and cozy just looking at her. She walked over to me slowly, then put her hand out like she wanted to pet me. I moved forward against her hand, and she ran it down my back. It felt so good. Then she picked me up, and it felt as nice as when my mom cuddled me and my sisters together at night. I looked up at her, and we smiled at each other.

Mistress must have been watching the whole time, because she walked over and asked the little girl if she would like to take me home. The little girl looked at me in wonder, and I, not knowing if she would say yes or no, meowed very softly right in her face to let her know that I had chosen her to be my family.

The little girl looked up at the lady and whispered, "Do you really mean it?" When the lady nodded, the girl spun me around in a circle saying, "Yes, yes, yes!" Lucky for me I was holding on tight.

Mistress smiled gently and said, "All right Amanda, let's go ask your mom."

Mom? Did she say Mom? Did this mean there was someone who could say no, and I wouldn't be able to keep my little girl?

Chapter 2

You bit the baby's what?

I NEEDN'T HAVE WORRIED. Amanda's mom turned out to love cats as much as Amanda did. And was she nice! When we got to my new home, she gave me a dish of cream, some tuna, and a nice warm blanket in the corner to lie down on if I got tired. But after I had finished eating, I was much too eager to explore to even think about sleeping.

Now remember, I had never been in a house before. My mom had told me a little bit about houses, but the barn was the only home I had known. I found myself in a small room with a big, soft looking thing in the middle that looked like a real challenge to climb. (I found out later that this was Amanda's bed.) It was covered in pink material that reached almost to the floor. I walked over to it, put out my claws, and jumped.

This was a big mistake. The pink covers were very soft, and my claws went in so far that they wouldn't come out again. So there I was, hanging by my claws, about a foot above the ground, and unable to go up or down. Since I couldn't think of anything else to do, I did what I had done all my life, whenever I got into trouble. I screamed, "Help me Mom!" at the top of my lungs.

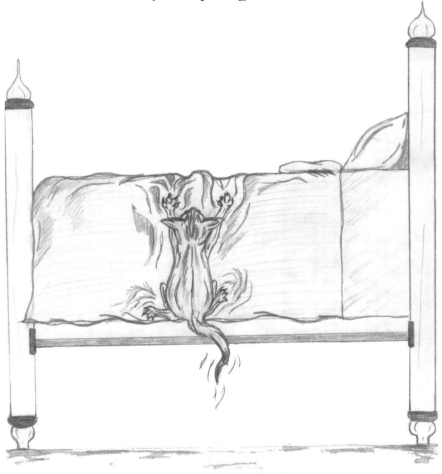

A moment later the door opened, and Amanda's mom walked in. "I thought I heard a meow for help," she said. She looked at me and bent to pick me up. "Silly kitty, if you want on the bed, all you need to do is ask," she said. She set me gently on top of the bed and started petting me. It was then that I realized I had a new mom to take care of me. I purred loudly to let her know that I appreciated her help, and the petting. After a few minutes, a strange, gurgling sound came from down the hall somewhere, and Mom went to check it out. I was on my own again.

From where I sat, I looked around the room. There were some funny looking animals all piled in one corner. They were made out of cloth, and I could tell they weren't real, but they looked worth checking out later. Over in the other corner was what looked like a miniature city. There were all these pretend people in a small house with cars, clothes, food, and shoes scattered all around. Most of the stuff was pink, and a lot of them had the same word printed across them. B-a-r-b-i-e. Barbie. I had never heard that word before, but I guessed maybe it was a code word meaning little people. I jumped down and tried taking a bite of a miniature ham that was sitting on a little table. Yuck! It was worse than chewing on my food bowl!

I was just making my way toward the cloth animals when that strange gurgling sound came from down the hall again. What could possibly make a noise like that? Only one way to find out. I walked out the door and started down the hall.

The hall was long and narrow with doors on both sides, but they were all closed. Besides, I could still hear that sound, and it was coming from the other end of the hall. At the end of the hall, I turned the corner and there it was. It was like the Barbies, only bigger. And moving. I froze to see what it would do. It started coming toward me very slowly.

It took me a moment to realize that it was a small human. A baby, like me! He was walking on all fours (I'd never seen a human do that before), and he was making little noises that sounded more like meows than human words. I tried to figure out what he was saying but gave up in the end. This language sounded half-cat and half-human but not enough of either for me to quite figure it out.

He was still coming toward me, but now he was putting out his hand like he wanted to pet me. I was very excited, because I figured that this would be a great new friend. After all, we were both little guys fairly new to the world; maybe we could explore the house together. He didn't have a tail, so we couldn't play 'Got your tail' the way I learned it, but he did have awfully thick cloth over his backside, so maybe that would work the same way. I moved forward slowly to let him pet me.

He touched me very gently at first. His hands were little, and a bit sticky, but he seemed to know that he was supposed to glide his hand down my back. But hold on! HOLD ON! I mean, LET GO! He had grabbed my tail and was holding on tight! At first I wasn't sure what to do. Then I realized he must be playing 'Got your tail,' and I reached around and bit into those baggy diapers of his.

15

Several things happened all at once. First of all, there was a nasty taste in my mouth, kind of like that miniature ham I had tried to eat earlier, only much worse. I also felt my teeth go a little farther than they should have and I knew they had gone into the little person's skin. If my teeth hadn't told me, my ears would have. That kid let out the loudest yell I had ever heard in my life. My ears still ring just thinking of it. He let go of my tail, and I jumped away to the other side of the room.

As soon as that yell was let out, Mom was in the room in an instant. She seemed to take in the entire situation at a glance and walked over to pick up the baby. She cooed sweetly into his ear and rocked him in her arms and he calmed right down. Then she walked over and sat down next to me and petted my back gently. "I see you met Andrew," she said quietly.

She placed the baby's hand on my back and gently pet me with his sticky little fingers.

"Now Andrew," she said, "you must never pull the kitty's fur or his tail. And Kitty, you must never bite or scratch the baby. If either of you has a problem with the other, just call me. You both know I'll come right away and take care of you. Now, are we all friends?"

Andrew and I looked at each other suspiciously. Then I meowed, and a big smile lit up his face. That was it. We were pals.

Amanda came home from school just then. She ran over

and picked me up, swinging me around the room. I was learning fast how to hang on.

"I think it's time we give that kitten a name," Mom said.

"You're right!" Amanda said. "How about Fluffy?"

"Nanonenananana," said Andrew. At least that's how it sounded to me.

"No Andrew, only black cats should be named Midnight," Mom said. Apparently she could understand this cat-human language.

"He looks like a mountain lion," Amanda said. "How about if we call him Leo?"

Mom looked thoughtful. "Do you remember that movie we watched last month about the mountain lion? What was that called again?"

"Charlie the Lonesome Cougar," Amanda said.

Andrew started jumping up and down. "Cha Cha Cha Chaeee!"

"Yea, Charlie would be a great name for him!" Amanda said.

I thought about it for a minute. Charlie wasn't a bad name. It had dignity (unlike Fluffy or Muffin or Fru-Fru or something like that), and it had a certain style that I kind of liked. I looked at Amanda and smiled.

"Charlie, do you like your name?" she asked me.

"Meow," I answered.

"Sounds like a yes to me," Mom said.

And that's how I got my name.

Chapter 3

The Monster from the Back Yard

THE ROOM I WAS IN was called the living room. I know that because that's what Mom and Amanda kept calling it. I looked around and noticed many pieces of furniture that would be fun to climb, but that could wait until later. I was still in explore mode. I noticed that Amanda and her brother had stopped talking and were focusing all of their attention toward one side of the room. I turned to see what they were looking at.

It was shaped like a window, and it seemed to look into another room. I could see people and animals all moving around quickly, so I went over to see who they were and what they were doing. As I got nearer, I could see that everything was smaller than normal. Just as I got up close, a cat danced right in front of me, holding a play mouse in its mouth. I couldn't resist. I reached up and tried to grab the mouse away with my paw.

I couldn't understand what was going on. My paw was right on that mouse, but I couldn't grab it. On top of that, the other cat didn't even seem to notice me, or the fact that I was trying to take his toy. He just kept walking around, doing this silly dance and meowing in a most peculiar way. And most puzzling of all, Amanda and Andrew were laughing their heads off behind me.

"Mom, Mom! Charlie's trying to catch a mouse off the TV screen!" Amanda yelled and laughed at the same time.

It was then that I realized that whatever this thing was, it wasn't a window, and the things on it weren't real. With as much dignity as possible, I turned away from this TV thing and wandered into the next room.

My luck was changing, because this room turned out to be the kitchen, which instantly became my favorite room in the whole house. It smelled wonderful! I couldn't figure out exactly what kind of meat was cooking, but I knew it was something good. Mom was standing in the middle of the room by a counter, working on something. I went over and rubbed up against her legs to let her know I was there.

She looked down at me with a smile. "Hello Charlie. Did that mouse on TV give you an appetite?" She walked over to a big door and opened it. I ran over and stuck my head inside to check out what was in there. It was cold, but oh boy, did that smell good too! I was just starting to identify a few of the smells (ham, cheese, milk, whip cream, and hamburger) when the door began to close, and my head

19

was still inside! I yelled as loud as I could and Mom managed to stop the door just an inch before my brain got squashed.

"Charlie, I didn't even see you. If you insist on putting your head in the refrigerator, it's going to get bonked." Mom walked over to the counter and poured some milk into a bowl, stuck it into a tiny door, pushed some buttons, waited until she heard a beep and then put the warm milk on the floor. It tasted great, so I drank the whole bowl. Then I started to get a funny feeling. Uh oh, time to test my memory of the house. Where was that litter box?

I managed to find the litter box and made my way back to the living room. Someone had opened the curtains and I could see that almost one full wall of the room was actually a glass door. I walked over to check out the back yard. It wasn't as big as the fields back at the ranch, but I could already imagine myself playing 'jungle kitty' in all that green grass. I was just checking out the flowers on one side of the yard when something hit the glass at about fifty miles per hour.

I jumped three feet in the air and two feet backward all in one move. I landed on the ground with my back arched, my fur up, and my teeth bared, hissing madly. I had only a vague vision of a huge brown monster pounding against the glass trying to reach me. Then I saw what looked like a gigantic tongue licking the glass, and a huge tail wagging back and forth so fast that my eyes couldn't keep up with it. Then I realized what it was. I had heard of them before, but I had never actually seen one. It was a dog.

"Mom, Frisky wants in!" I heard Amanda call. So that was its name. Frisky.

"All right, I'll let her in, but you had better hold Charlie. Frisky is very excited to meet him, but Charlie doesn't look too thrilled about the idea."

That was an understatement. I had no desire to ever meet that animal. But if we were going to share the house, or at least the back yard, I had better make its acquaintance.

Amanda picked me up and sat down on the couch. She held me very gently on her lap. The brown terror was in the house and almost on top of me within one second of Mom opening the door. And she was licking me. Every lick of that huge tongue washed half of my body. She licked one side, then the other, then the first side again. I think she might have actually eaten me all in one bite except Amanda kept telling her to be gentle. I tried to find something positive about the situation, but this huge washing machine was worse than both my sisters combined.

Finally I had had all I could take. I decided to try a new tact. "You can stop licking me now, I believe I am fully washed," I said very calmly.

"Huh?" The dog answered in a slightly dinghy female voice.

"I said you can stop licking me now. I am fully washed, in fact, I'm totally soaked!"

21

"Oh." That was all she said. It was clear to me that I was not dealing with a great mind. In fact, for all her size, this dog seemed downright stupid. This was an advantage I could use in the future if I could make friends with her and not get eaten.

"This is my first day here," I said conversationally. "Is it a good place to live?"

"Oh yeah!" she said in her slightly dizzy voice. "They're real nice here. They give you good food, let you play outside a lot, and take you for walks. Just don't bark at the neighbors, and you'll do just fine."

Like I was going to bark at the neighbors. Right. She started to lick me again, and I decided I would try to set some ground rules right away. I didn't want to get cleaned to death every time Frisky came into the house, and since I was still sitting on

Amanda's lap, Frisky couldn't bite me if she didn't like my ideas. "Please stop that!" I said in a firm voice.

To my surprise, she immediately stopped. So that was the key, she was used to responding to a firm command. "I would like to make an agreement about our living situation, if you don't mind," I continued. "I would prefer you don't wash me unless I actually need it. I would also appreciate it very much if you would be careful not to step on me. I saw the way you flew in the door, and if I had been on the ground, I would now be a part of the carpet. If you can do these things for me, I will try not to get in your way, and will keep my claws in my paws whenever you're around. Is it a deal?"

She looked at me very seriously, as if carefully thinking over everything I had said. Finally she said she would try.

I was doing so well with her that I decided to try for more. "I would also like it if you would share any extra tidbits of food you get from the table. I understand dogs get a lot of table scraps, and I've heard they're really good."

I had gone too far. Frisky's eyes got narrow and her body got tense. She looked me straight in the eyes and growled. "Don't you EVER touch MY food!" she warned.

If I hadn't been on Amanda's lap I probably would have been table scraps myself right then. As it was, Amanda yelled for Mom, Mom put the dog out, and I got a chance to collect my wits. I had gotten a good scare, but I also learned a valuable lesson. No matter what else you do, never ask a dog for its food.

Chapter 4

What's a Dad?

WITHIN A WEEK I had settled in and made the house my own. One of my favorite rooms was the bathroom. People spent an awful lot of time there doing an odd variety of things. It was not a big room, just large enough for the sink, a funny shaped chair, and a huge bowl that got filled with water every night for the kids. This bowl thing was called a bathtub, and it was my favorite place to get a drink of water. I have always had a 'thing' about water. It has to be fresh, and I mean really fresh, or I won't drink it. If it has sat in a bowl on the floor for more than five minutes, it is stale and tastes awful. I learned very early on that the faucet in the bathtub leaked. Therefore, there was always a few drops of fresh water in the bottom of the bathtub. I began to make a habit of getting all my drinks from the tub, and eventually the family caught on and just stopped putting bowls of water out for me. In fact, I once heard Mom say that she couldn't even think about fixing the leak in the bathtub, because I would probably die of thirst. That would have been true if I hadn't also learned to jump up to the sink to get a drink. If I sat up there and meowed long enough, someone would always come in, plug the sink and put in fresh water. It was great.

But this was only one reason I liked the bathroom so much. Another reason was that it was a great place to get some attention. Whenever someone was actually sitting down on that funny chair, I would walk up to them and rub against their legs. This would almost always result in the person petting me for the remainder of their time on the chair, and sometimes they sat there for a long time.

The family also did other strange things in that room. Mom would spend time putting funny colors on her face. Amanda called it make-up, and sometimes she would get into it and look just like a clown by the time she stopped. Mom usually yelled at her when she saw, and Amanda would have to take what was known as a bath. I had baths in the sink a couple of times and hated it. But Amanda and Andrew always seemed to enjoy themselves in there. The first time I saw them sitting in the bathtub, I assumed they were just in there getting a drink like I always did. I ran into the room and jumped into the tub with them. SPLASH! UGH! I hate water on my fur! And bubbles! There were bubbles all over my paws! I jumped out again as fast as I could and went running through the house with water and bubbles

25

flying all over the place. After that, I was always careful to check the tub before I jumped in.

There was one member of the family that I had not met yet. Someone called Dad was part of the family, but was away on something called a 'business trip' in someplace called 'Arizona.' Mom and the kids would talk to him every night on the phone and then talk to me about deserts and cactus. The first few days, I thought they were talking about some new kind of ice cream with special topping, but then I realized there was a difference between a desert and a dessert.

I got used to the routine around the house pretty quickly. Mom was always trying to keep the house spotless, but I would follow behind her to make sure the place still had that "lived in" feeling by moving my toys back to the middle of the floor. That way, they were much easier to find when I wanted them. Amanda went to school early every morning but came home in time for afternoon cartoons. Andrew played with Mom most of the day, but right after lunch he would go and take a nap, and one of my favorite times of day started. Mom called it 'break time.' We would sit on the couch together, and Mom would share her lunch with me and pet me while we watched TV or read. The shows we watched were really silly, and they hardly ever had any animals on them, but Mom liked them, and I liked being with Mom.

Then one day, this tall man came walking into the house

without even knocking. He took one look at me and said, "So you're the little furball I've been hearing so much about."

I wasn't sure if those were friendly words or not, but I was taking no chances. I ran to the living room and scratched on the back door to get Frisky's attention. After all, she was the watchdog, it was her job to take care of this stranger. But instead of barking and raising a fuss when she saw the man step into the living room, Frisky went wild with excitement.

"It's him, it's him! He's home, he's home!" she kept saying over and over in that dizzy voice of hers.

I was about to ask, "It's who?" when all of a sudden, Amanda and Andrew came tearing into the room screaming, "Daddy, Daddy! Hooray, Daddy's home!"

I looked this Daddy person over carefully. He was very tall and strong looking. He was smiling like crazy and hugging the kids and wrestling them to the ground, then they were all rolling around on the floor together in a big laughing, hugging pile. This looked like way too much fun to be left out of. I ran over and leaped on top of the pile.

Now, you have to remember I was only a little kitten. It wasn't my fault. After all, it takes a lot of practice to learn how to control your claws. I didn't mean to land claws first in the middle of Dad's back.

Dad jumped up with a yell. I was still holding onto his shirt with my front claws, but my back claws had let go, so I was dangling there in the air.

Andrew started laughing, then Amanda joined in. They were laughing so hard that Dad couldn't help himself and started laughing too. "Honey, come and get this fuzz ball off me!" he called to Mom between giggles.

"You're home!" Mom cried as she ran forward to hug him. But as she reached her arms around him, she felt me instead. "Either you're growing a tail, or you've just met Charlie," Mom said with a laugh.

She unhooked my claws and brought me around to face Dad. He looked at me very seriously and said, "I like cats, but you've made a pretty bad first impression here. However, you also seem to make my children happy, and that's very important. So I'll tell you what Charlie, I'll forget about this little mess, if you try to control those claws a little better. Is it a deal?"

I looked him straight in the eye. "Meow."

Dad looked very startled. I guess he hadn't really expected an answer. Then he started laughing again. "No wonder you guys like this little fellow so much. He's a smart one."

It was then that I realized people really like it when you talk with them. I began carrying on conversations with my family all the time, even though I knew they couldn't understand what I was saying. A typical conversation would go like this:

"Good morning Charlie."

"Meow."

"I had a great dream last night about a castle in the sky. Do cats dream?"

"Meow."

"I wonder what cats dream about. Chasing mice?"

"Meow."

"Sleeping in the sun?"

"Meow."

"Beating up dogs?"

"MEOW!"

Chapter 5

Christmas Trees are Not for Climbing

IT HAD BEEN ABOUT THREE WEEKS since Dad came home and things were going great. Dad started petting me whenever I would jump up on his lap, and he only stepped on me four or five times when he was getting into the refrigerator. The kids were very happy to have him home again, and Mom didn't seem as tired as she had been.

Dad also taught me a new game. It started out one day as he was checking all the flashlights and candles in the house because a storm was coming. He had carried a big flashlight into the kitchen and turned it on to check the batteries. When he clicked the little switch, a big, bright circle appeared on the floor in front of him. I watched that circle very closely, wondering what it could be. I had never seen anything quite like it before. As I watched, the circle suddenly moved and went right over my back and past me. I turned around to watch what it would do next, and it moved again. I decided to chase after it and see if I could catch it. I tried to grab the circle with my paws, but I couldn't get a hold of it. When it moved again, I continued the chase and pounced on it from behind. That's when I heard Dad laughing and turned to see what was so funny.

"Hey kids," Dad yelled, "come watch your cat chase the flashlight beam!"

I didn't know what he was talking about, but I noticed his hand move and saw the circle take off again. I chased it all over the room this time, and when it tried to escape by climbing up the wall, I jumped up after it. Dad was still laughing, louder and louder, and I thought he was making fun of me because I couldn't catch that darn circle. So I ran even faster, chasing it around and around, until I finally fell down, too dizzy to stand.

Dad came over then and picked me up. He was still chuckling to himself as he said, "Charlie, you are the silliest thing I ever saw." But after that, Dad got out a flashlight every couple of days, and I would chase the light around the room while he laughed. To this day, I still haven't been able to catch that dang circle, but it's good exercise!

Mom was the most popular person in the house. That doesn't mean that she was more loved than anyone else; I think everybody loved each other pretty equally. In the beginning, I thought everybody liked Mom so much because she was the one who fed us. After all, that was the first thing I liked about her. But after Dad got home, I realized there was something more. Mom was always hugging someone. Whenever she would sit down, there was a mad rush between Amanda, Andrew, and I to see who would get to her lap first. Whoever sat in her lap would get cuddled and hugged, and the other two would sit right next to her and snuggle close from the sides. Every night, she would read two bedtime stories. One she would read with Amanda on her lap and Andrew next to her, and one with Andrew on her lap and Amanda at her side. Whenever I got on her lap, she would pet me and nuzzle my ears and rub my neck. As soon as Amanda and Andrew went to bed at night, Dad would sit down next to Mom, and they would hug and cuddle. I started to figure out that hugging is very special and important. So I decided to learn how.

I tried it on Amanda first. After all, she was my special

person. She was sitting on the couch in the living room, watching TV. I jumped up in her lap as I always did, and she started to pet me. Then I surprised her. I slowly climbed up her chest, very carefully put one paw around each side of her neck and squeezed. I heard her gasp in surprise, and I thought maybe I had done it wrong and was hurting her. Then she reached her arms around me and hugged me back, saying, "Oh Charlie, I love you too!" and I knew I was doing it right. From then on, I made it a point to hug each person in the family at least once every day, just to let them know how much I cared about them.

It was in that third week after Dads return that I walked into the living room one day and saw the most amazing sight. Mom was standing in the doorway trying to pull a tree into the house. A real tree! The tree was much too big to go through the door, but Mom kept trying to pull it in. It didn't help matters that every time Mom moved, Frisky tried to jump through the open door to get inside the house. Andrew was sitting on the couch laughing like crazy, and I joined him there. So there was Mom, growling at the tree, yelling at the dog, and calling for Dad to come and help her when all of a sudden the tree got loose. It flew through the door, Mom landed on top of the tree, and Frisky landed on top of her. Dad walked in and started to laugh but thought better of it when he saw the expression on Mom's face.

Dad helped Mom up, carried the tree over to the corner of the room, and placed it in a stand. Then he brought a box that I'd never seen before into the room, set it by the tree and started pulling things out. I jumped down and ran over to check it out.

Dad began pulling long strings with tiny colored light bulbs all over them out of the box. I jumped out and tried to catch the lights as they went by. Suddenly I felt myself being picked up and lifted high in the air! I turned around and saw Mom looking into my eyes.

"I don't think you should be around while we decorate the Christmas Tree Charlie. You'd have way too much fun and make double the work for the rest of us." With that, she carried me to Amanda's room and closed me in. I wasn't happy about being left out of what looked like a great time, but, being a typical cat, I took it in stride by taking a nap.

About an hour later, Amanda came into the room to get something out of her closet and forgot to close the door when she left. As soon as she was out of sight, I jumped off the bed and sneaked down the hall to find out what was going on.

When I got to the living room, no one was there. I could see through the back door that everyone was outside playing ball. In the corner of the room stood the tree. It was the most beautiful thing I had ever seen. It had colored lights all over, balls in different shapes and sizes hanging from it's branches, long thin silver strings hanging everywhere, and a beautiful little girl with wings and a circle-hat on the very top.

I walked over to take a closer look. When I got right up next to it, I reached out a paw to touch one of the silver strings (I found out later that this stuff was called tinsel). It seemed to bounce away from my paw as I reached for it. This was better than chasing yarn! I started batting all the pieces that were close to the floor. Some of the strings came down, some just seemed to dance in the wind and stay attached to the tree, and some wrapped themselves around me. After a few minutes, I had gotten the strings off of all the lower branches, and I was almost covered in silver.

As I pulled the last piece I could reach down off the tree, I noticed that when I batted the branches, some of the pretty balls up higher on the tree were bouncing around. Aha, that could be fun too! But I couldn't reach any of the balls from the floor. The branches I was playing with weren't strong enough to hold me from the outside, but maybe if I got closer to the trunk I could work my way up. I decided to give it a try. I walked under the branches and across the silver and gold material that was laying around the bottom of the tree and made my way to the stand.

I looked carefully at the stand. I would have to step over it to get to the trunk. I put my foot on the stand to take a closer look and discovered, by having very wet toes, that there was water in the stand. So, I stepped very carefully over, grabbed a hold of the trunk of the tree, and started to climb.

There were a lot of branches coming off the trunk, so climbing was slow and difficult. I went about halfway up the tree and stopped. I couldn't reach any of the decorations from where I was, but some of the lights came right up to the trunk, so I could reach those. I started batting at a pretty red light, and it seemed to dance up and down as I played with it. The branch the light was on danced up and down too, and I could hear little bells tinkling from all over the tree. I started pawing harder at the light, trying to trap it in my paw, pretending it was a tiny mouse that I wanted for lunch. In fact, I got so carried away imagining that tasty mouse that when I finally caught the light in my paw, I bit right into it!

OUCH! I got such an electric shock that my fur was standing straight up! I jumped away from the light, completely forgetting that I was in the middle of the tree. I landed on the end of a branch, and the tree swayed slightly, then began to fall. Everything seemed to move in slow motion for the next few seconds. I could see the tree falling. I could hear the bells ringing. I could see Dad running through the back door, moving quickly toward the tree, but I knew he wouldn't be quick enough. I could see Amanda and Andrew outside the door, their eyes as big as saucers of milk and their mouths hanging open. And I could see the ground, rushing toward me so fast that I thought I could already smell the carpet. Then, at the last minute, it finally occurred to me that I had better move fast or I would be part of the pattern in that carpet, and I leaped to one side.

I landed the same instant that the tree did.

The next day there was a baby fence up all the way around the tree. I really hated that fence. Not only could I not climb the tree any more, I couldn't even reach the tinsel around the bottom. And a few days later all these pretty boxes with ribbons all over them started showing up under the tree, and I couldn't reach those either. Bummer.

The fence didn't come down until the day the family sat around the tree and opened all those boxes. That day was fun because everybody gave me the ribbons to play with, and Amanda gave me this toy mouse that ran around the room, and I could chase after it. It was a lot of fun, and I could bite it as much as I wanted without ever getting shocked.

I also got my first collar that day. It was green and had a little silver tag that had my name and address written on it. Mom put it around my neck and buckled it in place. I didn't like it. It felt weird having something besides fur around my neck, and the little tag jingled when I walked. As soon as nobody was looking, I used my back legs to push it over my head and off of me. Whew, that felt so much better. But then, as soon as Amanda spotted it on the floor, she put it on me again. And I took it off again. It became quite a game over the next few days, the family putting my collar on me and me taking it off again. I started trying to be clever and taking it off in places where they wouldn't find it. Under the couch, behind a chair, under the bed, in the potted plants, wherever I could think of. Pretty soon, my family got tired of looking for that stupid collar and just stopped putting it on me. I was really glad about that at the time, but later I would be very sorry.

Chapter 6

The Adventure Begins

IT WAS SPRINGTIME, and everything in my world was perfect. Now that the weather was nice again, I was allowed to go out back every day to play in the sun. I played 'tiger in the grass;' (this was especially fun if Dad hadn't got around to cutting the grass that week), and I pretended to be a great hunter. I used to imagine I was a huge cougar stalking prey in the forest. There were, unfortunately, no mice in our neighborhood, so I never learned to hunt for mice. Since I was a fairly small cat anyway, I learned to hunt bugs instead.

Bug hunting was one of my favorite things to do, and different bugs made for different levels of difficulty. Crickets were easy. We had lots of them in the yard in the early spring, and if I just sat still long enough, they would start singing and give themselves away. But that actually made them too easy to catch, and besides, they weren't very tasty.

Now beetles were different. They were much harder to catch and downright tasty when I actually got one. And grasshoppers were the very best. I had to be very slow and quiet when approaching a grasshopper, because if it caught sight of me, it could move ten feet away from me in one jump. This took not only patience, but expert pouncing skills as well. And when I caught one, they were a crunchy delight.

That's how my trouble all started. I was chasing a grass-hopper, slowly following it around the yard. It was getting close to the gate on the side of the house when I finally saw my chance to pounce. I crouched down, took careful aim, then leaped . . . and missed. The grasshopper jumped up on the gate and over the other side.

For the first time, I noticed the space under the gate. I could actually see that grasshopper on the other side, no more than two feet away from me. There was a spot over on one side of the gate where Frisky had dug a hole under-neath just big enough to put her nose through. If I flattened myself totally down to the ground and squeezed hard, I might be able to get out front and get that grasshopper. Unfortunately, it was a tighter squeeze than I imagined, and I let out a growl when my back scraped against the bottom of the gate. By the time I got all the way through, the grass-hopper had jumped into a juniper bush. I had learned long before this that junipers always pricked my nose, so I knew not to bother following him. Besides, for the first time since I lived on the ranch, I was free to go wherever I wanted. There was a whole world ahead of me, and I wanted to see what it was like.

I sniffed the front yard very closely before I went any further, so I could find my way back by the smell if I lost track of my direction. I decided to check out the neighbors house on the left first, as I had heard strange noises coming from that place over the back fence many times. As I approached the gate to their back yard, I heard a low growl coming from behind me.

"Grrr . . . who are you and what are you doing in MY territory?" It was an orange cat. A big orange cat. I mean a BIG orange cat! He had a scar on his ear and one on his nose that showed he had been in many fights and survived. He also had huge muscles all over his body that said he could smash me to tiny bits if he wanted to.

My heart was beating so fast I thought it would come out of my chest, and I tried to think of something to say. My tongue just didn't seem to work for a couple of minutes, but when it finally kicked in, "Hi," was all that came out.

"Hi? Is that all you've got to say before I kill you for being in my space?" he growled.

"But, but, but I live right next door there. See, th-that's my house," I pointed while I spoke. "I didn't mean to cause any trouble, I was just exploring out here."

"That house there is part of my territory," the big cat scowled at me while he talked. "I've never seen you out here before."

"This is my first time out of the backyard," I explained.

"Then this will be your last time. I'm not going to let you live there until you're full grown and decide you want to take over the front yard too." With these words he hunched down into pounce position and lowered his ears.

As you have probably guessed by now, I am not stupid. I knew I had no chance in a fight with this big cat; he would kill me in less than a minute. So I did what any smart animal in that same position would do. I ran like crazy!

The other cat was so surprised at my speedy take-off that it took him a few seconds to realize what had happened and to take off after me. By that time, I had a pretty good head start, but his legs were much longer than mine, so he was catching up quick. I thought about running back to the hole under the gate and getting to the safety of the backyard. No other cats ever went back there, because they never knew when Frisky would be out. But I knew it would take me too long to get into that little hole. If I tried, the bully cat would catch up and make a scratching post out of my backside while I was still climbing through.

So I kept running. I had no idea where I was going, and I got lost even more thoroughly because I kept running through hedges and other obstacles to slow down my pursuer. I must have run for at least three blocks before I saw something I thought could help me. It was a small box, sitting on the front porch of a large house. It looked like someone was in the process of building a birdhouse and hadn't hung it up yet. The door opening looked large enough for me to go through, but too small for the big bully behind me. I raced into it, scratching my back and sides as I went through the door, and curled up as small as possible in the farthest back corner.

The bully hadn't expected me to stop that quickly. He was smart enough to figure out he couldn't fit through the door, so he tried to turn to the side and go around the birdhouse, since he was going too fast to stop. He almost made it, but hit the corner with his nose and let out a fierce howl.

"Ow, ow, ow, ow. You rotten, no good kitten! My nose is going to be sore for at least a week, thanks to you. If you think you're getting away from me now, you're wrong." He reached his paw through the door and tried to scratch me, but his arm wasn't quite long enough to reach. I reached out and smacked his paw with my claws.

"OUCH! Why you little . . . well, you can't stay in there forever you little brat. I'll just wait right here and kill you when you come out." With that, he climbed on top of the birdhouse and sat down to wait for me.

I could hear him moving around above my head. It sounded like clean-up work, and I guessed he was licking his wounded nose and paw. I knew if I tried to get out of there now, he would be on top of me in an instant, and I would be a goner. I tried to think of what to do next, to concentrate on finding a solution to my situation, but I was so tired from the chase that I found myself drifting off to sleep.

It was dark when I woke up. At first I didn't know where I was, and I looked around to see if Amanda was asleep in bed next to me. Then I remembered. I was alone, in a birdhouse, far from home, and some big cat was outside waiting to kill me. I thought about going back to sleep to escape the problem, but that wasn't going to change anything. I had to use my brain and try to figure a way out of this mess.

I tried to listen very carefully to see if I could figure out what was going on outside. I could smell the bully cat, so I knew he was still out there. I could also hear noises coming from inside the house now, so the people who lived there were obviously home. I could hear dishes rattling and pans

44

clanking, so I assumed dinner was being cooked. Thinking about food made me realize how hungry I was. I hadn't had anything to eat except for breakfast and a couple of bugs, and that long run had used those up hours ago. My stomach growled and received an answering growl from the cat above my head.

Then an idea came to me. If I was that hungry, the bully must be hungry too. He had been sitting up there the whole day waiting for me to come out, so I knew he hadn't eaten either. Maybe, just maybe, I could use that to my advantage.

"Boy, whatever they're cooking in there sure smells good, doesn't it?" I asked.

"Yeah, it sure does," the bully replied. "Why don't you come out here and see if they'll give you some?"

"I think we both know what would happen if I did that," I answered. "After all, I'm stuck in here until I give up or you decide to let me go. But you aren't stuck. You could get some of that food pretty easily, I bet. Then at least one of us wouldn't starve."

"Yeah, you'd like that wouldn't you? For me to walk away and beg for food, so you could sneak out and run away while I'm not looking. Well, I'm not going to do that," he said in a nasty tone.

"But you don't have to move," I said slowly, trying to sound like I was thinking this thing through. "If you just meow really loud, the people inside will hear you. They'll think you're a poor hungry cat and will bring the food right to you".

"Yeah, it might work," he said, and started meowing as loud as he could.

Do you remember how I told you that I talked back to my humans all the time? Well, if you take the time to really listen to people when they talk to you, you learn a lot about them. I knew there were two possible outcomes from this big bully making a fuss on a stranger's front porch. Either they would really think he was a lost cat and bring him some food, or they would chase him away. I was counting on that second option.

"Here they come," the bully suddenly said. "Now you be quiet in there while they're giving me the food and I might not hurt you quite as much later." Wonderful, I thought sarcastically. He can only kill me once.

I could hear the front door open, and suddenly a deep voice boomed out into the night. "Hey you mangy, flea-bitten cat, get out of here. SCAT!"

Then I could hear footsteps coming closer and closer across the wooden porch. The big cat jumped off the top of the birdhouse and ran toward the sidewalk. I moved forward inside the birdhouse just far enough to see out, but not enough for anyone to notice me. I could see that big bully standing on the sidewalk, looking mad enough to chew nails. He looked like he would have waited there until the human went back into the house, but I guess the human figured that out too, because he started chasing the bully down the street yelling, "No cat is gonna hang around my house and try to kill the birdies," and, "I love birds, I hate cats!" and things like that.

I waited until the human came back and went into the house again before I crawled out of the birdhouse. But I didn't know if I was safe or not. That other cat could have turned around to come back after me as soon as the human stopped chasing him. It was also beginning to get late, and I knew there was no way I could find my way home in the dark. I needed a new hiding place, somewhere warm and safe for the night.

As I sat on that front porch looking around, I noticed the house next door. It was obvious that children lived there, because there were toys all over the yard. I saw a small pool like the one Andrew liked to play in at home, and I went over to see if it had any water in it. It did, and I took a long cool drink. It wasn't as fresh as I like my water to be, but at least it was clean, and after a long run and a bad scare, I really needed it.

When I had finished my drink, I took another look around. It was then that I saw the hole. It was a hole in the screen of an air vent leading into the garage. I hadn't been out in the garage at home very often, but I did know that inside is always warmer than outside, so I moved in for a closer look.

When I got close enough to the hole, I stuck my nose up to the vent to see if I could smell anything. I wouldn't want to go inside and find myself face to face with another bully cat or, worse yet, a cat hating dog. But there were no other animal scents in the air, so I slowly climbed through the screen and into the dark room.

It only took a minute for my eyes to adjust to the darkness. We cats see very well in the dark, so I could soon see the room quite clearly. Not that there was much to see. There were some cans against one wall, some rags piled up in a corner, but most of the room was taken up by the great big truck parked in the middle. It was a white truck, and the paint was kind of scratched up, which was funny to me since the sign on the side said, 'Paint Masters.' The back of the truck was covered with a hard shell, and when I jumped up to check it out, I could see more cans inside, plus a ladder and some paint brushes. The back of the truck looked interesting, but it was all sealed up and I couldn't get in.

I decided to check out the cans I had seen on the other side of the garage. Maybe there was food in them. I was getting very hungry after my long day, and even some of Frisky's dog food would have been welcome. I walked carefully over to the cans, but none of them had food, they were all full of paint.

Still hungry, but very tired, I walked over to the pile of rags in the corner and laid down. I fell asleep and dreamed I was a bird, hiding in its house from a big cat, and eating dog food.

Chapter 7

A Wild Ride

I WOKE UP TO THE SOUND of a door being opened not far from me. I flattened myself against the pile of rags as much as I could so as not to be noticed. A big man came into the garage and opened the back of the truck. He put a bag inside and loaded some of the paint cans from against the wall into the truck. Then he turned around and went back into the house, leaving the back hatch of the truck wide open.

After he went inside, I stood up to stretch for a minute, listening carefully for any sound of the man's return. I began to smell something. Something good. Something to eat. I followed my nose to the back of the truck, and realized what it was I was smelling. Tuna fish! My favorite food in the whole world! I was so hungry that I didn't even think twice, I just jumped right up into the back of the truck.

The tuna was in the bag the man had put in. I used my

paw to open the bag, and realized it was the man's sandwich I was smelling. For a moment I paused. This food wasn't meant for me. Eating it would be like stealing this man's lunch. I took a deep breath and just savored the smell of the tuna. Oh, it smelled so good. Maybe he wouldn't mind if I just took a little bite. After all, I was a starving little kitty, how mad could he get? And besides, I'd make sure he never saw me to figure out who to blame.

I climbed into the bag and began removing the wrapper that was around the sandwich. I took a big bite. It tasted wonderful. Tuna, mayonnaise, and just a touch of garlic. Heaven!

I was so busy savoring my first bite that I didn't hear the man come back into the garage. I was all the way into the bag when I suddenly heard him right near me, putting more paint cans into the truck. I stayed absolutely still, figuring I would run out and try to find home as soon as the man went back into the house. Only this time, the man closed the back of the truck and I was trapped inside.

I heard a woman's voice call from the house, "Goodbye George, have a good day. Don't forget to pick up milk on the way home."

"No problem Honey," the man named George called back. Then I heard the engine start up and the truck began to move.

I must take a moment here to tell you that I absolutely hate riding in cars. Up to this point in my life, I had only gone for three car rides. The first trip was when I went home with Amanda for the first time. That would have been okay, except that I was very sad about leaving my mom. The second and third car rides I took were both to the same place. The Vets. The vet is this big man with cold hands who smells like a dog and gave me all kinds of painful shots. After my first ride to the vet I cried and tried to get out of the car the whole way home. On my third trip, I cried both ways and, I'm ashamed to say, I actually bit Mom when she tried to get me into the car.

So, needless to say, I really freaked out when I heard that truck engine start. I no longer cared about being spotted, I just wanted OUT. I ran to the back window and started yowling at the top of my lungs.

But George liked country music. And George liked his country music LOUD. I could hear it all the way in the back of the truck, but George couldn't hear me. Normally, I really would have enjoyed that music, but right then all I could think about was escape.

In another moment I realized I had other problems to deal with. At the first stop sign we came to, George really slammed on the brakes, and I went flying into the tailgate. Oh, my poor nose! Then he took a quick turn, and I went flying into the side of the truck. Then a left. Then another right. Then another quick stop. Wham, wham, wham. I just couldn't get a grip so I wouldn't go flying. I tried to put out my claws, but they just slid across the metal with me, making an awful scraping sound in the process.

51

Then the paint cans started moving. It seemed like we would go around a corner, I would fly across the truck and hit the wall, then the paint cans would come chasing after me and try to smash me. It was kind of like a demolition derby, and I was the car everybody wanted to smash first.

Finally, after what seemed like hours, the truck stopped in front of a house. I was still laying on one side, surrounded by paint cans, when I heard George coming around to open up the back. Quick as a flash, I was on my feet and crouching at the tailgate. When he opened the back of that truck, I was out and running down the street in the blink of an eye. "What the . . . what in the world was that?" I heard George saying as I disappeared around the corner.

Once I was free from the truck and safely out of George's reach (I still wasn't sure if he would be mad about that tuna sandwich), I hid behind a bush and tried to figure out what I should do next. I had no idea where I was, or which direction to go to get home. It seemed like we had traveled for miles in that truck, but for all I knew we had been driving in circles the whole time.

I started licking my fur to straighten it back in place and to check if I was seriously hurt or not. I could feel a lot of bruises under my fur, but nothing that wouldn't heal within a day or so. My biggest problem was going to be getting home. I tried to think hard about what would be the best thing to do. If only I had my collar on! Then I could go up to any friendly looking person, and they would know by my tags who I belonged to and would call my family. Unfortunately, my collar was still under the slide in the backyard, where I had hidden it the last time I took it off.

That's when I remembered the time I had been sitting with Amanda, when Mom had talked to her about what to do if she ever got lost. They had been about to go to a parade, and Mom wanted her to understand how important it was that they all stay close to each other. She had told

Amanda that if she did get lost, not to go running around and looking for her, but to find a policeman and he would make sure she got home safely.

A policeman! Brilliant! All I had to do was find one and let him know I was lost. Policemen have a way of figuring things out (I knew this from watching TV with Mom and Dad), so I was sure one would know who I belonged to and how to get me home.

Now all I had to do was find a policeman. I started walking down the street, trying to figure out the best place to look for one. The neighborhood I was in was full of little houses, but everything was quiet and peaceful, so I didn't really think a policeman would be out just walking around. I had seen policeman on TV walking around on busy streets with lots of big buildings, or out directing traffic, but there wasn't anything like that around me. So I just kept walking, hoping to either see signs of home or a policeman.

I walked a long time. About two hours later I had seen no signs of anything familiar or of a policeman anywhere. In fact, I had seen very few people at all, and the ones I had seen were all busy going somewhere or doing something, and they didn't even notice me as they walked past.

Then I saw a little girl. She was standing in front of a small house. She had on a dirty pink dress, and her hair, which was dark brown, was falling in her face. But she had a big smile on her face, and she was looking straight at me. She ran over to the front porch and grabbed something off a chair. Since she was still looking at me, I watched to see what she was getting. She started walking toward me, then stopped about five feet away. I was just about to run, to make sure she didn't try to grab me, when she held out a piece of sandwich for me to take. I guessed that it was a part of her lunch that she just hadn't eaten yet.

Normally I would never accept food from a stranger. That was another rule I had heard Mom talk about, and I figured that it was as important for cats as it was for kids. But the only food I had eaten for a day and a half now was a few bugs and that big bite of tuna sandwich. I walked a little closer, so I could smell the sandwich and see what kind it was. I was hoping for tuna, but I wasn't too disappointed to find out it was peanut butter. Andrew had given me bites of peanut butter before, so I knew it was good stuff.

I went a few steps closer and stopped. I really wanted that sandwich, but I figured it was a good idea to be cautious. I thought the little girl understood, because she set down the sandwich and stepped back so that I could get it. I walked over to the sandwich and took a bite. Oh my, it tasted so good. I hadn't realized how hungry I was. I forgot all about where I was and what I had been through and just savored every morsel of that sandwich. It was just what I had needed until . . .

HEY! LET GO OF ME! The little girl had grabbed me around the middle and picked me up into the air. She was squeezing me so tight I could hardly breathe. Then she opened the door and carried me into the house.

Chapter 8

The Tea Party

Up until that time, the little girl hadn't said a single word. As she carried me into the house, she opened her mouth and started yelling to her mother. After that, I can't remember a time when she wasn't talking.

"Mommy, mommy, I found a kitty! He's all alone and hungry and nobody owns him and he really needs me and I'm gonna keep him for my very own! Okay mommy?"

"Yeah, yeah, whatever honey," came the answer. We had come into a living room, and I could see a woman lying on the couch reading a magazine. She never even looked up, but added, "But you're responsible for any mess he makes, you understand?"

"Oh yes Mommy. Yes, yes, yes. Thank you, thank you, thank you!" Then she carried me back into her bedroom.

It was a small room, with a big bed in the middle and broken toys tossed all around. It was such a mess that, even when she sat me down a few minutes later, there was hardly room for me to walk.

But she didn't put me down right away. First she had to tell me a few things. At first I just laid there in her arms listening, not believing that one little girl could talk so much.

"My name is Mary Elizabeth Sutton and I'm five years old. My favorite color is pink. I love dolls and stuffed animals and dressing up and playing tea party. I used to have a bunny named Marly and I used to pet him all day long, but then he bit me and Mommy made him go live someplace else. My favorite food is peanut butter sandwiches and chocolate milk. If you're very, very good I might share some of my food with you. This is my room and these are all my toys. This is my bed and that is my dresser and that is my closet and that is my desk and those are my clothes."

She finally took a breath. I had been trying to answer back like I was used to doing with Amanda, but she never stopped long enough for me to get a meow in edgewise. Just as I was opening my mouth to say something, she started in again.

"Your name will be Sara, and I'm going to dress you up and we will have a tea party this afternoon."

Sara? Someone needed to let this girl know that I was a boy.

I tried. "Meow."

"What did you say? You want to get dressed right now? Okay." With that, she grabbed a doll's dress and started putting me in it.

A moment later, there I sat. In a pink dress with frilly lace on the bottom and a big bow in the back. She tried to put little white shoes on my paws, but they kept falling off, so she settled for little white socks trimmed with lace. I was so embarrassed.

She kept talking the whole time she dressed me, and continued to talk while she walked away to set up the tea service. She kept telling me how happy we were going to be together and how much fun we were going to have. All I could think of was how much I missed Amanda and Andrew and how I wished I would wake up and find that this was all a bad dream.

But it wasn't a dream, and I decided that enough was

enough. While Mary Elizabeth set up the tea table, I used my back paws to push the dress off over my head. Then I pulled the lacy socks off with my teeth and threw them on the floor. I was just starting to feel like myself again when Mary Elizabeth came back to take me to tea.

"What have you done!" she screamed. "Oh, you naughty thing you. You are a bad, bad kitty, and I'm going to have to punish you now."

She picked me up and carried me over to the closet. "Now you just stay in there and think about what you did, you bad, bad kitty." Then she threw me in the closet and closed the door.

For the first few minutes, I was a little upset. After all, you only get called a bad kitty if you do something really wrong, and being locked in a closet was pretty serious punishment. Mom would never have done that to me. But after a while, I began to relax and curled up on some clothes that were lying on the floor.

I could hear Mary Elizabeth through the door. She was still talking, to her dolls now, and the tea party was proceeding just fine without me. I was actually quite comfortable there in the closet, and I settled down for a catnap, glad that I had gotten out of that dress and the party.

I woke up a short time later when Mary Elizabeth opened the closet door.

"Oh, my kitty! I forgot about you! I'm not mad at you anymore, and my dollies and I were just about to take a

59

walk, so you can come with us. Just let me get the baby stroller and we'll be on our way."

She picked me up and put me into a pink doll stroller, then stuck three dolls on either side of me. That being done, she covered us all up with a thick blanket and wrapped it so tight that I couldn't move any of my legs.

So there I was, with a doll arm digging into one side of me and another doll's leg on top of my tail, and Mary Elizabeth talking a mile a minute as she strolled us through the house and out the door. I might have been stuck there for a long time if Mary Elizabeth hadn't gone crashing down the porch stairs the way she did. The impact of each step knocked me and the dolls this way and that, until we all lay in a jumbled heap by the time we reached the bottom step.

Now that I was free of the blanket, I peeked out of the doll stroller to see where we were headed. Unfortunately, we were going back the same way I had already come, and I didn't want to go that direction again. As Mary Elizabeth turned around a corner, I leaped out of the stroller and started running the other way.

"Sara, come back kitty!" I could hear her yelling behind me. But there was no way I was going to put up with her nonsense and non-stop talking for another minute. When I realized she was chasing after me, I started running full speed and had left her far behind within a couple of blocks. I kept running though, just in case. In fact, I kept running for at least ten blocks, turning several corners, always making sure I wasn't going in circles, until I figured there was no way that little girl would ever find me again. Every time my legs started getting tired, I would remind myself what it would be like to live with Mary Elizabeth for the rest of my life, and I would run another three blocks.

Chapter 9

Two Very Strange Characters

AFTER RUNNING FOR ABOUT TWO HOURS, I came to an area with lots of side streets and alleys with very small houses and apartment buildings on them. The streets smelled of garbage, but by then, I was so hungry that even that smelled good. I kept my eyes open, I was still looking for a policeman to help me, and this area looked like a place where I could find one. I can't quite explain why, but that neighborhood made me very uncomfortable and scared. My heart was beating as fast as it had when I was hiding in the birdhouse. The only thing I can say is the streets just felt mean.

Pretty soon, I was walking through a dark alley when I saw a coffee can sitting next to three garbage cans. As I walked by, I could see that rain water had collected at the bottom of the can. It was dirty. It was rusty. It was water, and if I didn't have a drink soon, I wouldn't be able to walk any further. I took a small drink. Oh man, did it taste nasty.

As I sat there, drinking filthy, smelly water, I thought about how many times I had made Mom drain the sink and put fresh water in because what was there had sat for ten minutes. I never realized how lucky I was to have my family until then, and boy, did I want to get back to them!

As soon as I had finished my drink, a new smell came to me. Somewhere, in the garbage cans next to me, there was food. I jumped up onto the closest can and smelled around some more. I caught a faint smell of some kind of fish in the middle can, so I carefully reached my claws under the lid and pushed it over to the side. I looked into the can and started pushing gross, moldy garbage around, trying to find something I could eat. There was an old fish-head next to some lumpy cottage cheese, under an old lunch bag, and I started to reach down to grab it when I heard a voice from close by.

"What do yous think you're doin' in there?"

I looked down and saw two very straggly looking cats. One was big and skinny, the other one was small and skinny. They both had dirty, knotted fur and scars on their ears. They were also very strong. I could see that by looking at their legs. They reminded me of a lion's legs, all muscle under the fur, ready to spring into action whenever necessary. I hoped I wouldn't have to see them at work.

I was very nervous as I looked down at them. I wasn't sure what to say, so I just went for honesty. "I was hungry," I said in my best 'look, I'm still just a kitten' voice.

"And yous decided to have a snack out of one of OUR cans, huh?" The little one asked.

"I'm sorry. I didn't know these were yours. I'm lost and I was just trying to get enough food to see me through until I can find my way home."

They both looked me over very carefully. "So yous don't knows where you are then, or who runs this territory?" the little one said. When I shook my head no, he said, "Claude, this guy may be da answer to our little problem."

The little cat seemed to be in charge since he kept doing all the talking while the bigger one, Claude, just stood by watching. "Hop on down here, little guy. This may be a lucky day for all of us."

I jumped down next to them, watching very closely to see if they were going to pounce on me. I kept remembering my experience with the bully cat, and I didn't think I'd be able to find any birdhouses in this neighborhood.

"My name is Clyde, and this here is my partner Claude. What's your name little guy?"

"M...m...m...my name is Charlie," I said, stuttering on my words in fear.

"Ah, don't be scared Charlie; we're not gonna hurt ya. We wanna be your pals, ain't that right Claude?" Clyde said, looking over at his big friend and winking.

"Yeah, yeah sure. Whatever yous say Clyde," was Claude's only response.

"Charlie here looks very hungry Claude. What say we takes him over to some of our better cans and get him somethin' decent to eat, alright?"

"Yeah, sure thing Clyde," was all the big one said again.

I wasn't sure why they were being nice to me, but I wasn't in any position to turn down food. Especially decent food. These guys still made me very uncomfortable, but as long as they weren't out to hurt me at the moment, I had no real choice except to go with them.

They walked me down three blocks and then over two more until we came to the back of a building with a sign on it that read 'Vito's Restaurant.' The garbage cans there were overflowing, and the food had just been dumped that afternoon. There were scraps of meat and vegetables and noodles everywhere, and I pigged out on all the meat I could find. It tasted so good after going without for so long. Clyde and Claude just watched me eat, only taking a bite now and then, which I thought was strange considering they both looked more starved then I was.

I finally stopped when my stomach couldn't hold any more. What I really wanted at that moment was a warm place to curl up, clean my face and fur, and go to sleep. But my two new "friends" were waiting for me to finish, and I knew I had to face them. I could hear them whispering to each other, making plans, but I couldn't hear what they were saying. I turned around and jumped down from the trashcan I was in and looked at Clyde and Claude.

They were wearing big smiles on their faces, but they weren't nice smiles. They were more like smug grins, like they had just figured out how to catch a bird that had been bothering them for months. Somehow, I felt like the bird.

"Well, thanks a lot guys. I really appreciate you showing me this place and letting me eat here. I'd better start looking for home again." I said this as I started walking away from them, hoping it really was "good-bye."

"What's your hurry Charlie? I thought you were lost. How you plannin' on findin' home?" Clyde asked.

"Well, I thought if I found a policeman, he could help me find my way," I explained.

"Oh, no. Don't do dat. Don't ever do dat!" Claude got a panicked look on his face. I had never seen a big cat look scared, and this guy looked terrified. "Don't go to the police. Tell him Clyde! Tell him!"

"It's okay, Claude, it's okay," Clyde tried to calm the big cat down. After a moment he turned to me. "Yous sees

Charlie, if you go to a cop, or if a cop catches you, they will takes you to da pound. Da pound is where all animals that don't belongs to no humans go. They keep you there a few days, then they sends you to kitty heaven. Do yous understand what I'm tellin' yous?"

"You mean they kill cats?" I asked in absolute horror. Claude nodded his head.

"But, I do belong to a human. I have a family."

"But you don't have no collar," Clyde looked pointedly at my neck.

"I . . . I . . . I lost it."

"But you sees, without no collar, the pound don't know who to call to come and claim you. So after a few days inside a steel cage, its wings and harps all da way."

Suddenly I couldn't move. It was almost impossible to believe what they were saying was true, but somehow I knew that it was.

"So maybe yous ought to rethink your plans Charlie," Clyde continued. "We, Claude and I, have a slight problem which yous may be able to help us with. If yous do a good job, we's could let you hang around here with us until you decide what yous wants to do."

For a moment, I didn't answer. All I could do was sit there and realize that I had no way to find home. The police had been my only hope, since I had long since figured out that I was very far from home. I sat there, feeling totally alone for the first time in my life.

Then I remembered something Clarise had told me long ago. Each of us has a purpose in life, a special talent. I hadn't found anything very special about me yet. Maybe I shouldn't go home. Maybe I belonged here. These two cats seemed to think there was something I would be able to help them with, and they had only just met me. Maybe this is where I belonged, out on the streets, on my own, a wild cat. I liked the sound of that, *wild cat*. It sounded independent. Free. In control of my own destiny.

Lonely.

If nothing else, I needed time to figure out who I was and what I was going to do with myself now, and these guys were offering me the time and space to do that. All I had to do was one little favor for them. "What do I have to do?" I asked.

Clyde and Claude smiled at each other. "Well you sees, Charlie," Clyde began, "there's this cat over on Baker Street, goes by the name of Ralph. Every week, we delivers five mice to him. It's sort of a little agreement we's has. But this week, me and Claude couldn't catch enough mice to deliver any extras to Ralph. We just want yous to go to Ralph, and let him know that we won't be makin' our delivery this week, and we ain't sure when we'll be makin' another one. If ever. Yous thinks yous can remember all that?"

"Of course," I told him. It made perfect sense to me. It was obvious that these two could hardly catch enough food to feed themselves, let alone be giving food to other cats. It didn't occur to me until much later to question why they were bringing food to this Ralph fellow, or why they even bothered with mice when they had that great garbage bin behind the restaurant.

Clyde and Claude were smiling again. That same smug smile. It made me uncomfortable, but I thought the best thing to do would be to earn their trust by doing them this favor. Maybe then they would smile real smiles.

Clyde gave me directions then on how to find Ralph. It wasn't very far away, and I wondered why they didn't go and talk to him themselves, but I figured they were just doing me a favor by letting me help them. So off I went to find Ralph Cat.

Chapter 10

King Ralph and the Big, Mean Dog

BAKER STREET WAS IN A BUSY SECTION OF TOWN. There were lots of cars, shops, and people. It was the kind of street I had been looking for only hours before. I even saw a policeman standing on the corner, but I knew better than to go anywhere near him. In fact, I stayed as far away from him as I could, and ran past when his back was to me.

Clyde had told me to look for a small alley next to a bakery. That was where this cat, Ralph, was supposed to live. As I walked along, I could smell the bakery. It smelled of sweet breads and creamy butter, and I thought of the cream Mom used to give me.

I shook my head to chase away those thoughts. That was the past; I was starting my new life today, and I knew I would never be happy if I kept thinking about my old one.

I slowed down when I reached the bakery, looking very carefully for the entrance to Ralph's alley. I spotted it and began walking in. I made it about two feet when a large cat jumped in front of me and growled, "Who goes there?"

"I'm looking for Ralph. M...m...my name is Charlie, and I have a message from Clyde and Claude."

The big cat looked me over very carefully. I guess he decided I was harmless, and he moved his head to point which way to go.

Suddenly I was very uncomfortable. Why was there a guard at the entrance to the alley? Who was this Ralph anyway?

I went between a long row of trash cans to the very back of the alley, which turned out to be a dead end. There, in front of the back wall of the alley, sat a very large, very fat cat. He was a tortoise-shell tabby, with dark stripes and swirls from the point of his nose to the tip of his tail. There were girl cats on either side of him, very attractive and constantly preening themselves. In front of him sat three big burly cats, like guards. I could see that no one got close to Ralph unless Ralph wanted them to.

"Who are you, and what do you want?" Ralph said in a bored voice.

I took a deep breath. "My name is Charlie. Clyde and Claude asked me to come and see you. They asked me to explain to you that they're very sorry, but they won't be able to make any more deliveries to you in the foreseeable future."

"WHAT?" Ralph seemed to explode. The girls on either

side of him ran and hid behind some boxes that were in the corners. "Do you have any idea WHO I am or WHAT you just said to me?"

"N...n...no," I stammered.

"I am King Ralph, Boss of the whole East Side. Everybody on this side of town has to do what I say, when I say, or they get beat-up by some of my boys, like these you see in front of me," he pointed to the three big cats who were sitting below him. They smiled at me like I was cat food and flexed their muscles.

King Ralph was looking closely at me while I stared in horror at the big cats. "You really didn't know who I was or what you were walking into, did you?" I nodded my head, still afraid to look away from the big cats who I expected to jump over and kill me at any moment. "I can tell," King Ralph continued. "What exactly did Clyde tell you?"

"He just asked me to deliver the message. He told me that they deliver five mice a week to you as part of a deal you have with them. They said they couldn't catch enough mice this week, so they didn't have any extras to give you," I explained.

"And just what did they promise to do for you in return for delivering this message?" Ralph asked.

"Well you see, I was lost. They gave me some really good food and told me I could stay with them until I figured out how to get home."

Ralph looked me over very carefully, then nodded his head. "I believe you kid. Let me explain my 'agreement' with Clyde and Claude. They are required to bring me five mice a week if they wish to continue living and hunting within their territory. If they do not bring the mice, I send some of my boys to make sure they leave this end of town forever. Clyde does not like this arrangement, and Claude does not know how to think, so he goes along with whatever Clyde says. They have given me trouble before, but they always delivered the mice on time. Sending you was their way of telling me that they no longer intend to honor our agreement. They knew I would have them punished on the spot if they came themselves, so they sent you. I'm sure they expected you would be punished here and now, and that might increase the amount of time before I got around to finding them. Fortunately for you, and unfortunately for them, I am a cat of superior intelligence and I took the time to hear your story. I know you are not responsible for what you said to me.

"Tuffy, Spike!" Ralph called out the names and suddenly two huge cats appeared. "Go over and pay a visit to Clyde and Claude. Let them know they are no longer welcome to live in this area, and that if I ever catch them on the East Side again it will be the last day they ever see. Make sure you are firm with them, if you know what I mean." Ralph held up one of his paws like a fist, and the two cats nodded their heads and smiled nasty, cruel smiles, then they took off running back the way I had come.

I just stood there, wondering what was going to happen to me next. Then suddenly Ralph looked at me as if a new realization had come to him. "I just remembered something you said kid," he started. "You said Clyde and Claude gave you some really good food. Where did they get this really good food?"

"From a dumpster behind Vito's Restaurant," I explained.

All of a sudden there was a very angry look in King Ralph's eyes, and one of the girl cats who had come out of hiding gasped and ran behind the box again. "I wish you hadn't told me that kid. You see, that is my personal favorite dumpster. No other cat is allowed to eat out of it. I know you were unaware of this, but if I let you get away with it, others might think they could get away with it too. So now the question is, what kind of punishment is appropriate? If you were a cat from within my territory you would be killed

74

instantly, but that would be unfair in this instance. Hmm," he rubbed his chin with his paw as he gave the matter serious thought. Then he smiled. "I believe a dog fight is in order."

I felt my heart begin to beat loudly and my eyes grew wide. I didn't know what he meant by a dog fight, but I knew it couldn't be something good.

From around me I heard several voices begin laughing and cheering, and I realized there were now at least twenty other cats in the alley, and they had all been watching everything that had happened between Ralph and me. They began to climb up on the boxes at the back of the alley, and one by one they jumped over the fence. Suddenly the three huge cats that had been sitting in front of King Ralph were standing all around me, pushing me toward the back fence and forcing me to jump over.

On the other side of the fence there was an open field, closed off by fences on all sides. Nothing was growing there but some dead grass, and in the center of the field, there was a large pit. The other cats had all gathered around the pit, and that was where the bodyguard cats were now pushing me.

When we got right next to the pit, I looked down. It was about six feet deep, with straight dirt sides that were too steep to climb. At the bottom of the pit there was a dog. A big dog. A big mean dog. A big mean dog who looked like he hadn't eaten in a long, long time. He was black and white, with beady black eyes and a short tail. All the cats were yelling down to him, calling him names and teasing him for being trapped in the pit. With every word the dog looked madder and madder, until all you could hear was his loud growl, and all I could see were his big teeth.

"Attention everyone," Ralph called out, silencing all the cats. "We will now have a contest between this cat, who made the very large mistake of eating out of my dumpster, and Killer the dog. It is appropriate to remind everyone present that Killer here is undefeated, and has made snacks out of every one of his opponents to date. Bets will be taken now if anyone wishes to bet on the cat, and I will pay five mice for every one bet if the cat survives." No one bet on me.

I felt myself being pushed closer to the edge of the pit and decided it was time to try reasoning with King Ralph. "Please sir," I begged, "reconsider. I didn't know I was doing anything wrong. I'm not even one year old yet. Don't I deserve another chance?"

"I am sorry kid," Ralph replied. "But if I let you off the hook, the cats around here might think I was going soft. And there is nothing soft about King Ralph!" This last part was growled to all the cats standing around, and they all bowed low before Ralph to acknowledge his power over them.

Then Ralph nodded his head toward me, and one of the

bodyguards pushed me over the edge and into the pit.

I hit the ground hard, and when I looked up, I found myself face to face with Killer. This was a very uncomfortable position, as I was looking straight into a huge set of teeth. Killer drooled, licked his lips, and said "Ah, lunch."

There was no place to run. The pit wasn't very big, with no corners to hide in and walls too high to jump. As Killer moved toward me, I could only see one place to go, so I ran right between his front legs, under his stomach, ducked down low to go under his tail, and ended up behind him.

As Killer turned around to face me, I ran too, staying behind his tail as he turned in circles trying to catch me. After a few times around, I could see he was beginning to get very dizzy from turning in circles, and I was tired of getting hit in the face with his tail. That's when I got my idea. I kept turning him around and around until he looked like he was about to collapse, then I leaped forward and landed all four paws worth of claws right on Killers bottom. I bit him as hard as I could in the tail end, then jumped up on his back and from there leaped out of the pit in one quick move.

Killer was howling, and it had all happened so fast that the cats watching didn't have time to react. I ran past them, jumped over the fence, and ran out of the alley as fast as I could. I don't know if any of them tried to follow me or not, but I kept running for the next two hours, never looking back.

Chapter 11

All's Fair at the Fair

I SPENT THE NEXT TWO DAYS WALKING AROUND, finding food and water where I could. Food mostly consisted of bugs, which there were plenty of, but I soon discovered that cockroaches are very tasteless, and their legs get caught between your teeth. I was downtown now, walking past big buildings and stores. After what Clyde and Claude had told me about the police, I was afraid to be seen by anyone, so I mostly walked at night and found small corners behind garbage cans where I could sleep during the day. I was careful never to open or even sniff at any of the garbage cans I went near, so no other cats bothered me.

Everyday I got sadder and sadder, as I missed my family more and more. When I slept, I would dream of home. I would see Mom cooking in the kitchen and feeding me little pieces while she worked. I would see Dad playing 'chase the flashlight' with me while Rock and Roll music played in the background. I could hear Andrews's laughter as I chased him around the living room. But mostly, I dreamed I was in Amanda's arms, and she was hugging and petting me. Each time I would reach out my arms to hug her back, but I would only feel cold sidewalk beneath me, and I would wake up, still alone.

I still had no idea what my special purpose was, but I knew I wasn't cut out to be a street cat.

Then one day, as I was walking down yet another alley, I heard children laughing. The sound was coming from behind a tall hedge that ran along the entire block. It sounded so sweet and wonderful that I decided I just had to see the kids who were doing all that laughing. I found an opening under the hedge and climbed through.

The sight that met my eyes on the other side of that

hedge was amazing. The laughter I had heard was coming from three kids who were having a picnic on the grass with their Mom. They were sitting in the middle of a huge field of grass, and there were lots of other picnickers all around them. Beyond the field was a great open area that was covered with colorful tents, trailers, machines, and about a million people. There was a big banner across the front of one of the trailers saying, 'Welcome to the County Fair.'

As I stood there by the hedge, just staring at all the incredible things that were going on, the children I had first heard laughed again. I looked over and saw that one of them was a little girl. She had long blonde hair and blue eyes, and seemed to be about the same age as my Amanda. I knew it wasn't Amanda, but since I didn't expect to ever find my family again, I thought maybe this little girl could love me the same way Amanda had. I walked up to the corner of their picnic blanket, sat down and meowed softly at her.

All three kids turned to look at me as soon as I spoke. There was a boy about nine, the little girl was about seven and a smaller boy around three. They looked almost exactly alike, with hair the color of straw, blue eyes and skin so light it was almost pink. If the little girl didn't have longer hair and they hadn't been different sizes, I might have thought they were triplets.

"Hi Kitty!" the girl said. She reached over to pet me, and I leaned into her hand to let her know that I liked what she was doing.

"Where did he come from?" the mother asked. I looked up at her and found she looked exactly like the children, only older. She was looking all around, trying to see if someone had lost me.

"He's so neat!" said the older boy. "He looks just like a mountain lion. Can we keep him mom?"

"He must belong to someone," the mom said. "I'll tell you what, we'll keep him with us while we walk around the fair and see if anyone comes to claim him. If not, we'll notify the lost and found booth and take him home."

"Hooray!" All the kids yelled. They yelled so loud that it hurt my ears, but I was glad to be going home with someone. It would be nice to sleep in a house and eat real food again. I was very tired of living on the street.

"Well, what shall we do next?" the mom asked.

The kids yelled, "The rides! The rides! The rides!"

It was really funny. These kids not only looked alike, their voices sounded almost the same, and they said everything in unison. It was like having three stereo speakers surrounding you, with one voice coming out from all three directions. I didn't know what 'rides' were, but I was anxious to be a member of this new family, so I figured I would do whatever they wanted.

We went over toward the big machines I had seen in the distance before, with the mom in the lead, the kids trailing behind in single file, and me in the little girls arms. As we got closer, I could see there were kids all over each one of these 'rides.' There were rides that looked like miniature cars all going around in a circle, one that looked like a giant spider with kids hanging from each arm, little trains that took people down twisty, turning tracks really fast, and a giant loop that turned the kids upside down. There was lots of screaming and yelling going on all around us, but everyone seemed really happy, so I guessed these things must be fun, even if they didn't look that way to me.

"What ride shall we go on first?" the mom asked.

"How many do we get to pick?" the older boy wanted to know.

"Each of you pick out one ride for all of us to go on," the mom answered.

"Want horseys, want horseys, want horseys!" the little boy yelled.

"How about you Cynthia?" the mom asked the little girl.

"The Ferris Wheel," the girl holding me replied.

"And I want the roller coaster," the older boy said.

"Okay, the merry-go-round is first," the mom said as we headed for the ticket booth.

We got in line, and I looked at this merry-go-round thingy. It was a pretty big machine, with little play horses all over it that went around and around in circles. As we got on, Cynthia, the girl who was holding me, picked a blue horse with golden stars on its saddle and climbed up on top of it. I kind of liked it up there. As I looked around I could see way out across the whole fair, and I felt like a very important cat indeed. After all, how many cats travel by horseback?

Then we started to move. Up, down, up, down, then around and around and around and around, all the while still going up, down, up, down. I held on to Cynthia as tightly as I could without digging my claws into her. We seemed to be moving really fast, and as I watched the world spin by, I started to get very dizzy. I got so dizzy that I thought I was going to lose my lunch and still we kept going up, down, around, and around. I looked up at Cynthia and meowed pitifully, but she was laughing so hard she couldn't hear me. Why is she laughing? I thought. This was no laughing matter. This machine was some kind of torture chamber!

Finally, the thing came to an abrupt stop. Cynthia jumped down from the horse, jolting me yet again as she held me in her arms. I wondered how long it would take before my head stopped spinning up, down, around and around.

"Now the Ferris Wheel!" Cynthia shouted.

The kids all ran over to a line by this giant circle that was spinning around. Oh no, I thought, not more circles!

Luckily, the line was long and my head had stopped spinning by the time we got into the little car and they closed the seat belt around Cynthia's lap.

"If you insist on taking him, you better hold on tight to that little kitty," the man who was running the machine said.

"You wouldn't want him to jump away from you when you're at the top."

I looked up to the top of the machine. It was so far over my head that I couldn't even imagine being up so high. He thought I might try and jump from there? How stupid did he think I was?

The ride wasn't bad when we started. We just went a few feet and stopped, a few feet and stopped, as they loaded and unloaded kids from each car. But when we stopped at the top, I got scared. We were miles above the ground from what I could see, and Cynthia's big brother was rocking the seat back and forth, so I felt like I would fall to the ground at any moment. Then the machine started and didn't stop. We began going around and around and around in a giant circle. Faster and faster and faster until the whole world began to look like one big blur that got bigger and smaller as you got closer or farther away. Every time we started down, it looked like we were going to smash into the ground, and then suddenly we would be pulled backward and start up the other side again. I began to get dizzy, and Cynthia and her brothers started laughing again. That's when I realized that this was not the family for me. If this is what these guys considered fun to do with your cat, I wanted no part of them.

Then the ride came to a stop with us up near the top again. Slowly, one car at a time, we worked our way back to the ground. I knew I had to make my move the moment

84

we reached the bottom. Cynthia hadn't let up her tight grip on me since she had first picked me up, and I knew I was going to have to be a bad kitty to get away. But I had no choice. I couldn't live this way, and I knew I wouldn't be a good pet for these kids if I was unhappy. We were definitely not a good match.

The minute our car stopped at the bottom, I let out a loud "MEOW!" and put my claws into Cynthia's arm. I didn't scratch hard, but it startled her so much that she let go of me. This was what I had hoped for, and I leaped from the car and started running before Cynthia and her brothers were even unbuckled.

When I hit the ground, I was really moving, and I started running through people's legs and around machines and buildings until I felt it was safe to slow down. I stopped to rest under a trailer that smelled like hot dogs.

Whew, that had been a close call. I might have made it all the way home with those kids and been trapped in their house before I found out that getting sick was their idea of fun.

Chapter 12

Horse Sense

IT WAS COOL AND COMFORTABLE under the hot dog trailer, so I settled down for a nap and stayed there until after dark. When the fair quieted down and everyone had left for the day, the people inside the trailer left also. As they left, they dumped their garbage into a trash can right behind the trailer. After they were gone, I sneaked over to the can to take a peek. I had been smelling hot dogs all afternoon, and I was really hungry! The trash can had a lid on it, so I stood on my back legs and stretched my front legs as high as I could, until I could push the lid off with my front paws. Then I jumped up to take a look at what was inside.

Hot Dogs! Dozens and dozens of hot dogs! Most of them were overcooked or broken into pieces, but they were the best tasting food I had ever had in my entire life. I ate and I ate and I ate until I felt like my stomach would burst. While I ate, I thought about other times when Amanda had fed me bites of her hot dogs. She always said they were her favorite food, but they had only been okay with me. Until now. Now hot dogs were the greatest food ever created, and if I had the power to vote I would make sure a statue was built in honor of the man who invented them.

When I finally jumped down from the trashcan, I took another look around to decide where to go next. There was trash piled everywhere, and as I looked, some of the trash seemed to move! I kept watching until I figured out that it wasn't the trash that was moving, but mice. This seemed to be mouse heaven, because there were hundreds of them, everywhere, eating all the garbage laying around on the ground. I was glad I was so full from all the hot dogs I had eaten, so I wasn't forced to try to catch any of the little things. They were so busy eating that I probably could have caught one really easily, but, to tell you the truth, the idea of eating a mouse really didn't excite me. I mean, bugs are one thing, but all that fur in my mouth? No way.

I decided to head over toward the lights at the other end of the fairgrounds. There was nothing much to see around the machines and trailers now that they were all closed, and the picnic area on the grass was empty except for what was left for the mice.

As I reached the last row of trailers and came out the other side, I began to catch a vaguely familiar scent. I took a deep breath to try to identify the smell. (Sniff, sniff) sweet hay. (Sniff, sniff) fresh oats. (Sniff, sniff) cow pies. A barn!

I looked up and could just make out several long buildings in the dark. I headed toward them, hoping to meet some friendly animals. As I got closer, I could see that the buildings were actually long, open stalls, with different types of animals in each row. I went past the cows. I had never made friends with a cow, because their stalls always smelled much worse than anybody else's. I went past the pigs, as I had always found them to be very ill-mannered and self-centered. The goats and sheep held no interest for me as I passed by their stalls because, let's face it, goats and sheep are stupid. But when I came to the last set of stalls, I got very, very excited. Horses!

I walked down the row of stalls, looking up into each one to see if any were friendly enough to talk to me. Most horses like to have cats around, because we keep mice out of the barn, and mice always try to steal the horse's oats. But most of the horses were sleeping. I guessed that they had probably been put through their paces all day in horse shows. Clarise used to tell me about the competitions she was in when she was young, and they had sounded like a lot of work.

I walked up to one stall where a young horse was looking out over the gate, and I said, "Hello."

"Do you know how to get me out of this stall?" the horse asked me. "I really hate the way this place smells. The cows are stinking up the whole area, and no one is taking care of the problem, so I've decided to leave."

"I wish I could help you," I said very sincerely. "But I don't see how I can. I don't believe I could get that latch on the gate open for you, and I climbed under a hedge to get into this place. There's no way you could get out the way I came in."

"Then leave me please. If you can't help me, I would rather be alone." Then he stared off into space, pretending I was no longer even there.

Well, that was depressing. Here I was hoping to have a conversation with an intelligent animal, maybe even make a friend. Instead I just get snubbed for being too small to help someone escape. Like I didn't have problems of my own!

I continued walking down the row of stalls, hoping to find a less depressed horse to talk to. As I passed one of the very last stalls in the line, I heard a voice behind me. "Charlie?"

I turned to look and just about fell down from the shock. It was Clarise! My dear old friend from my days as a kitten in the barn!

"Clarise, is that really you?" I asked in surprise.

"Well now, who else would it be?" she answered with a big smile.

"I can't believe it! This is great! But what are you doing here?" I asked in wonder.

"Mistress decided I might have one more blue ribbon left in me, so she entered me in the show this year. After looking over the competition, she's decided I may have several ribbons by the time we leave," she said proudly.

"Wow, that's really great Clarise," I said with pride for my friend. Then I remembered something. "Hey, you called me Charlie! How did you know my name? I didn't have it yet when I lived in the barn."

"From your mother, of course. She has kept very close track of you and your sisters since you left home. Whenever she sees your little girl's grandfather coming to visit, she runs for the main house and sits there for hours, listening for just the slightest word of you and what you are up to. She is very proud of you and boasts to all of us about the success you've made with your new family." Clarise was smiling, but then a puzzled look crossed her face. "But Charlie, what are you doing here? There aren't any houses near the fairgrounds, so how in the world did you get here?"

"It's a long story," I said. Then we both got comfortable, and I told her everything. From my first day at Amanda's, how I got lost, and all the trouble I'd been having ever since.

Clarise was very understanding. "Now Charlie, there is only one answer. You must go to the police at once and let them help you."

"But I don't have my collar on. Claude and Clyde said they kill cats whose owners don't claim them at the pound." I was really feeling tired. Just talking about what I had been through the last few days had totally worn me out. "Besides, I haven't figured out my special purpose yet. Maybe I'm not supposed to be somebody's pet."

"Haven't figured out your special purpose!" she said in surprise. "But of course you have, Charlie. All right, let's examine the situation. When are you the most happy?"

"When I'm sitting on Amanda's lap and she's petting me. Or when Mom is talking to me in the kitchen, and every time I answer, she gives me some tuna. Or when Andrew is chasing me and trying to grab my tail, though I don't like it when he actually does catch it. Or when Dad is playing flashlight with me. Or . . . ."

"That's enough. Now Charlie, tell me what you are especially good at doing."

"Well . . . ." I thought about everything I knew how to do. From hunting bugs, pouncing, digging, eating, sleeping, talking, and thinking my way out of dangerous situations. But what was I the best at? "Making people smile. I know each one of them so well, I can make any member of my family smile, even when they're sad."

"And doing that makes you happy, doesn't it?" Clarise asked.

"Yes, it makes me very happy," I said.

"There now, that was easy, wasn't it? Your special purpose is to make your family happy. It's as plain as the nose on your face. Or the nose on my face, which is much, much bigger!" Clarise said with a laugh. "Now all we have to do is get you home."

"Which takes us right back to where we started," I said.

"Charlie, you said your family loves you right? Don't you think they are looking for you?"

"Well, yeah. I guess they probably are."

"And where do you think they will be looking?" Clarise asked.

"Not here. They'd probably never think to look for me here."

"I think you're right about that. But do you think they will be looking everywhere they can think of? Wouldn't that include the pound?" Clarise was smiling as she said this last part.

"Well . . . YEAH! And if they're checking with the pound . . . ." I started to say.

"And have turned in a missing animal report . . . ." Clarise interrupted.

"Then they'll find me there for sure!" I finished with a cheer. Then my smile disappeared as another thought came to me. "But what if they don't check the pound?"

"They will Charlie. They love you, and I knew from the moment that little girl saw you for the first time, she would never be parted from you if she could do anything to prevent it. Now don't think any more gloomy thoughts. It's almost daylight. Go find a policeman, outside the fairgrounds, and make sure they get you to the pound as soon as possible. I bet I know a little girl whose heart is just breaking every day that passes without knowing what's happened to you."

"I'll never be able to thank you enough for everything you've done for me Clarise."

"No thanks are necessary. You just go on home and have a happy life. That will be thanks enough for me," Clarise answered with tears in her eyes.

"Say hello to my mother for me!" I yelled as I ran back toward the hot dog trailer. I knew I could find my way back to the hedge and out of the fairgrounds from there.

Chapter 13

Excuse me Sir, you have powdered sugar in your eyebrows

I FOUND MY WAY OUT OF THE FAIRGROUNDS without any problems and headed back towards the busy streets I had passed the day before.

I looked for a policeman for over two hours. And to think I had been hiding from these guys for days! Now that I wanted one, there wasn't a policeman in sight.

Then I remembered something I had overheard some people talking about. It was a joke on a TV cartoon show that Andrew had been watching. These turtles had been laughing about how policemen like to hang out at doughnut stores. I didn't know if it was true or not, but I decided to give it a try, and I followed my nose to the closest doughnut shop.

It smelled great sitting in front of that store. I was there for about five minutes when a patrol car pulled up in front of the place and one of the policemen got out. He was about to walk in the door when I looked up at him and said, "Meow."

"Hi Cat," he said. Then he just walked in the doughnut shop. He didn't even stop. He didn't ask me if I was lost, or if I needed help. Well, I would just have to try harder to get his attention when he came back out.

I watched through the window as the officer bought doughnuts and coffee. When he started to come out of the store, I stood right in the doorway and said, "MEOW!"

"Look out cat, comin' through!" he said as he stepped over me.

Now I was beginning to lose my temper. I needed help and this guy was completely ignoring me! Then I smiled, as an idea came to mind.

I ran forward and put myself between the policeman and the patrol car. Then I stepped in front of him and rubbed up against his leg just in time to make him trip! He landed face first in the box of doughnuts, with coffee spraying in every direction.

When he got up, he really looked mad. I figured he would be so furious he would put me in handcuffs and take me straight to the pound. That's what I wanted. Instead, he started laughing!

"Oh man, this is gonna' be one of those days, huh Frank?" he said to his partner in the car.

"It looks like it," the officer in the car answered. "Climb on in. You can get cleaned up while we drive around. Any of those doughnuts still good?"

The first policeman brushed off all the crumbs, gave me a funny smile, then climbed into the car. I couldn't believe it! All that and they still weren't taking me with them?

It was time for action. I heard the police car start up and decided on my next move. Taking careful aim, I jumped through the open window and into the back seat of the police car just as it was taking off. The officers didn't notice me at first. They kept talking about the smashed doughnuts, and that they would have to stop later for more coffee. I finally got tired of waiting for them to notice that they had company.

"MEOW!"

"What the .... Hey Lou, we got a passenger!"

"How in the world . . . . Hey, you're that same cat that made me fall into the doughnuts. Are you some kind of troublemaker?"

"Meow."

"Hey Lou, it sounds like he was answering you! He got a collar on him? Maybe we could get him to his home."

"No collar Frank. What's the matter little kitty, are you lost or something?"

"Meow," I said sadly so they would understand me. I was actually feeling very excited because someone was finally trying to help me!

"Ah, poor little thing. You're so pretty, you've got to be somebody's special pet. Hey Frank, what say we stop by the animal shelter and see if they can find this guy's family for him, huh?"

"You got it Lou," Frank answered with a smile. Then I smiled. I climbed into the front seat and onto Lou's lap and snuggled against him to let him know that I really appreciated his help. He stroked my back and rubbed my ears, and I felt happy for the first time in what seemed like a very long time. "You know what Frank? I'm gonna check back with the shelter in a week or so. If they haven't found this little cat's family by then, maybe I'll take him home with me."

Chapter 14

Life Behind Bars

THE POLICE CAR STOPPED in front of a long, low building. It was small and gray and very depressing to look at. Lou carried me inside and went up to a lady standing at a window. He explained how he had found me, where he found me, and that he wanted me if my owners couldn't be found. That made me feel better. At least I knew that if my family didn't show up, I would have a place to live other than kitty heaven.

The lady wrote up a report and thanked the officers. Then she carried me through a narrow door to the back.

The smells that came to me the minute that door opened sent me into a panic. I could smell dogs, lots of them. Big ones, small ones, hurt and sick dogs. And other cats. I could not only smell all the dogs and cats, but I could hear them. Most of them were crying, some because they were sick, some because they were scared, others because they were confused or lonely.

The other smell in the place was even worse. It was cleaners, lots of them, like the kind they use at the vets office. The aroma of animals and sickness and disinfectant all mixed together to create an awful smell.

"Here's another new one for the found section, Lill. What do you want me to do with him first?" the lady who carried me in asked.

Lill was a very large woman with enormous hands that were at that moment holding down a poodle and scrubbing its ears. She answered the question without even looking up. "Flea dip," was the only thing she said.

"Oh, but Lill, this one looks very clean," the lady who held me stated.

Lill looked up from the poodle with a disgusted expression on her face. "I don't care if that's the most pampered cat in the world, who has taken a bath every day of his life. Every animal that comes in this place gets dipped, first thing, then shots. If we were to let even one flea in this place, we would be overrun by the little critters within a week. And if we let one of these animals come down with rabies or something while they're in our care, this place would be shut down before you could say 'Health Department.' Dip him."

"Okay, okay. I was just asking." The first lady carried me into the next room and sat me down on a table while she put on a raincoat. I thought that this was a very strange thing to do since it was a beautiful, sunny day outside. Not that you could tell from inside that room. There were no windows in the entire building, just gray walls. It could be snowing outside, and I wouldn't know it.

When she picked me back up again, she looked me straight in the eye. "Now kitty, you're probably not going to like this, but it has to be done. Now, don't do anything either of us will regret, like trying to scratch me or something, okay?"

With these words she carried me over to a huge garbage can. I had no idea what was going to happen until she opened the lid of the can, and I could see the foamy, white water inside. It smelled awful, like the stuff Mom used to spray on anthills in the back yard. Then the lady held me up by the scruff of the neck, and pushed me into the water.

I couldn't believe she was actually doing this to me! She pushed me all the way down, until only my eyes and nose were up out of the water. She even twisted my head around so my ears would go under. I thought I was done for, that she was going to drown me right then and there, and I would end up with wings and a halo after all. Then, miraculously, she pulled me out! She wrapped me up in a towel and rubbed my fur to get as much water out as possible.

But I wasn't about to trust her again. I was mad now. I had gone with her willingly and not put up any kind of fight, but that was over. When she tried to pick me up again I hissed at her.

"Now kitty, it's all right. The bad part is over. All you need is your shots, and then you can have a nice rest."

No way. I knew the word 'shots,' and I knew I had had all of them that I needed. There was no single way I was going to let this lunatic stick a needle in me.

She walked over to another table and picked up a long needle. She turned around with it in one hand, and as she approached the table I was sitting on, she reached out her other hand to grab me.

I let her hand get right up by my head, then as she reached to grab the scruff of my neck, I let her have it with both paws. Ten claws, all razor sharp from my recent adventures, bit into her hand before she knew what was happening.

"OUCH!" she yelled. She pulled her hand back, dropped the needle from the other hand and grabbed a towel to stop the bleeding. When she looked over at me, I lowered my ears, arched my back, and growled at her. I wanted her to know that she should be ready for a lot more of the same treatment if she tried to give me a shot again.

"Oh forget it," she said, "it isn't worth it. I'm sure you already had all your shots, and I'm not getting hurt again for nothing. I'll just tell Lill that you're ready." With that, she left the room, still holding a towel wrapped around her hand.

Lill walked in a minute later. She looked very stern when she came through the door, yelling for that other lady to watch the front desk while she took care of me. But as soon as the door closed behind her, she changed. A large smile came over her face, and she suddenly reminded me of a big, friendly grandma. "Why, you're an abyssinian!" she cried. "Aren't you just the most beautiful thing!" I looked down at myself. I was still soaking wet from my flea dip, and I was rather skinny after spending so much time on the street. If she thinks I'm beautiful now, I thought to myself, she's going to flip when she sees me dry.

She picked me up very gently and started rubbing my ears and neck. I started to purr, very softly at first, then louder as she began to stroke my fur all the way down my back. Even wet and scared, it was so nice to be liked for just who I was.

"I bet someone is missing you very much," she said, as she continued to pet me. "I'll put you in the holding area with the others, then I'll check the missing pet reports right away. You should be very easy to identify. I wonder what happened to your collar?"

All right already, all right already, I thought. Enough about the collar. I've learned my lesson, I swear!

She carried me out of the room then, and through a long hallway past several large doors. I could hear dogs barking and cats yowling behind each of those doors, all sounding sad and hopeless. When she came to a big red door, she opened it and carried me through.

Inside were rows and rows of metal doors. They stretched all the way down both sides of the corridor, which was longer than some of the alleys I had walked down. Lill reached down to a small door on the bottom row and pushed me through, and then she latched the door behind me.

It was a cage. A cold metal cage just a little larger than I was, so I barely had room to turn around. Inside the cage, there was nothing except a small bowl of water and another bowl with some nasty tasting cat food in it.

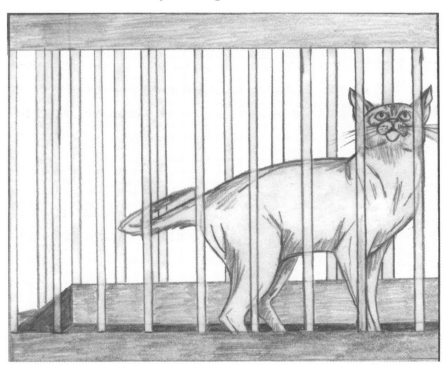

Before I even had time to figure out what was happening, I heard Lill say, "Now don't you worry little darling, I'm going to go check the lost pet lists right now." Then she went back out through the red door.

I looked carefully around me. I realized the cages were

stacked on top of each other, piled four high, so when I looked up, there were three other cats over my head. This was not a comfortable feeling since there were no litter boxes in the cages, and I could only imagine what would happen when the cats above me had 'accidents.' There were cats on each side of me, stretching for rows and rows and rows. Not all the cages had cats in them. There were some dogs at the other end, and some of the cages were empty, but I figured there were at least seventy-five animals in that one room.

When we had first walked in the door and all the animals had seen Lill, things had gotten very quiet. But as soon as Lill left, all the animals started talking at once, and I almost didn't hear it when the cat above my head started talking to me.

"So, what are you in for, pal?" He asked with a laugh.

"What do you mean?" I asked him.

"Sorry, that's an old line from prison movies. I used to watch them with my special person all the time. My name is Fluffy. Please don't laugh. The old man I lived with gave me that name, because his favorite pastime was to brush and pet my long fur. He was a great guy. He died last week, and since no one else in his family could take me in, I was sent here to either find a new family or . . . ."

"Please," I said quickly, "let's not talk about the 'or elses' around here."

"I understand. It's a very difficult subject for all of us

here," Fluffy said. "By the way, what's your name?"

"Charlie. It's very nice to meet you, Fluffy. I hope you don't mind me saying this, but I hope I'm not here long enough for us to become too close of friends."

"Well, don't feel bad about that. None of us like it here. That black cat next to you for instance. Blackie is his name." The black cat in the next cage smiled at me while Fluffy kept talking. "Blackie came in here and expected to be claimed within the first hour. He's been here almost a week now."

"If someone doesn't claim me soon, it's curtains for me." Blackie said in a strangled tone. "All I did was go for an outing. You know how it is. We're cats, for goodness sake. We go out for two or three days at a time, then we go back home. But when I got home, my family had moved. They're just gone. The new owners called the pound, and I figured my family would come here to find me. And now . . . ."

"Just don't think about it Blackie," Fluffy said in a soothing voice. "Go back to sleep until some more people come in looking for new pets." Blackie curled up into a little ball and hid his head under his paws to go to sleep.

Blackie's story had upset me. What if my family had moved? What if they lived far away now and never even thought of me? What if that nice policeman forgot about me too? In a week, I might be worried about . . . .

"Charlie, you can't let things like that worry you this early in your stay," Fluffy said, seeming to read my mind.

"If you do, you'll go crazy. I've already seen several cats carried away, never to be brought back, some of them before their week was even up, just because they went crazy and started biting the people who feed us. Try to relax. Think of this as a little vacation. Nothing to do but eat and sleep for as many days as it takes." Fluffy smiled at me then, but I could see that all the time he was trying to comfort me, he was also trying to reassure himself.

"I think I'll take a little nap now," I said. With any luck, maybe I could sleep until my family got there to pick me up. If they got there.

Chapter 15

There's No Place Like Home

I WAS STILL SLEEPING. It had taken me awhile to get to sleep in that uncomfortable wire cage, but once I was asleep, I had the most marvelous dream. I was home. I was playing with Amanda. She was holding her long hair in front of me while I sat on her lap, and I was trying to catch it between my paws. Mom was in the kitchen cooking. I could hear her as she put pots on the stove, and I could her the microwave beeping. Andrew was on the other end of the couch, reading a story with Dad. It was all so peaceful and fun, and then I heard Mom's voice calling from the kitchen. "Charlie . . . Charlie?"

I opened my eyes. Mom was looking into the cage with a huge smile on her face.

"Meow?" I asked, wondering if I was still dreaming.

"Oh Charlie, it is you! Over here you guys!" she called. Suddenly the whole family was there. Amanda was laughing and crying at the same time. "Oh Charlie, I missed you so much! You had me so worried!" she cried.

"MEOW!" Let me out! I wanted to be in my family's arms right then. I still couldn't believe they were really there, and I didn't want there to be any chance that they would leave without me.

"I'll go tell them up front that he's ours. Don't worry kids, someone will be right back to let him out," Mom said happily.

Amanda, Andrew, and Dad stayed with me while Mom went out the door, and they started telling me all they had done to try to find me. I could feel the tears in my eyes when I realized how hard they had been looking and how worried about me they had been.

When Mom came back, the lady who had given me my bath was with her. "Oh, this one," she said when she saw me. "He gave me quite a hard time. Never did give him his shots, so I'll make sure you're not charged for those. Do you want to take him out of the cage yourself? I've already got as many of his claw marks as I'd like, thank you very much!"

She opened the cage, and Dad reached inside to take me out. He held me for a moment, snuggling me against his strong warm chest, then he leaned down and let Amanda and Andrew pet me for a moment. Then, to my surprise, he put me in a box!

"MEOW!" No, Dad, don't do this to me!

"It's okay Charlie," Amanda was saying. "We have to carry you out in a box; it's the rules."

Didn't they know, by the way I'd acted about the shots, that I didn't care about the rules in this place? I had been waiting for days to be held and petted and loved by my family, and now they were putting me in a box!

Dad closed up the top, and I could only see through the little holes in the sides. We walked back out through the red door, and I meowed good-bye to Fluffy and Blackie. Then we walked down the long hall, back to the front desk where Lou, that nice policeman, had turned me in. As Mom paid the bill they gave her for taking care of me, I heard her asking where I had been found. When they checked the paperwork Lou had filled out, Mom said she couldn't believe it, that I had been over twenty miles from home! We walked out of the pound and to the car.

When we got in the car, Amanda opened the box, and I climbed out onto her lap. As she started petting me, I looked out the window and watched as the small, gray building called 'The Pound' disappeared behind us. I hoped I never had to see it again. I rubbed up against Amanda and started purring. Thank goodness I had a family that loved me.

I didn't enjoy the car ride home. I didn't like being in the car any more than I ever had, and I kept meowing at Dad, trying to explain that I would much rather walk home. But as we kept on driving and kept on driving and kept on driving for over thirty minutes, I realized I had been very far from home indeed.

When we finally got home, I ran from room to room, looking at everything and smelling everything and rubbing up against everything to make sure nothing had changed. Nothing had. Then I went to the kitchen, and Mom gave me some tuna and a bowl of warm milk. It tasted better than ever, and I almost choked trying to purr and eat at the same time.

Later that day, after I had eaten and been petted by everyone in the family several times, Mom and Amanda announced that they were going shopping and would be back in a little while. I decided it was a good time to take a nice long nap on Amanda's bed while they were gone. Andrew came in every few minutes, checking to make sure I was still there. I wanted to explain to him that I couldn't get lost in the bedroom, but I just accepted the fact that he had missed me as much as I had missed him, and I went back to sleep.

When Mom and Amanda got home a short time later, Amanda came to the bedroom and carried me back to the kitchen where everyone was gathered. Mom said she had a surprise, and that Amanda had picked it out especially for me. She opened the sack and took out a beautiful new collar. It was white leather, with little red stones all around. And in the middle was a bright red heart made out of metal. It was a tag. It said 'CHARLIE' in bold letters, with my phone number underneath.

"Now Charlie," Mom looked at me very seriously as she hooked it around my neck, "we expect you to keep this on."

She didn't need to say it. I've never even considered taking it off.

Want more of Charlie?

Check out the sequels:

Charlie Moves to Arizona
Charlie and the Rodent Queen

Coming in the Fall of 2004:

Charlie Goes Camping

If you want to order additional copies of this book, they are available on our website **www.charliethecat.com**, or send $6.95 plus $1.00 shipping and handling to:

GoodyGoody Books
P.O. Box 1073
Sun City, AZ 85372